AASHI

KSHAMA

Made with ♥ on the Notion Press Platform
www.notionpress.com

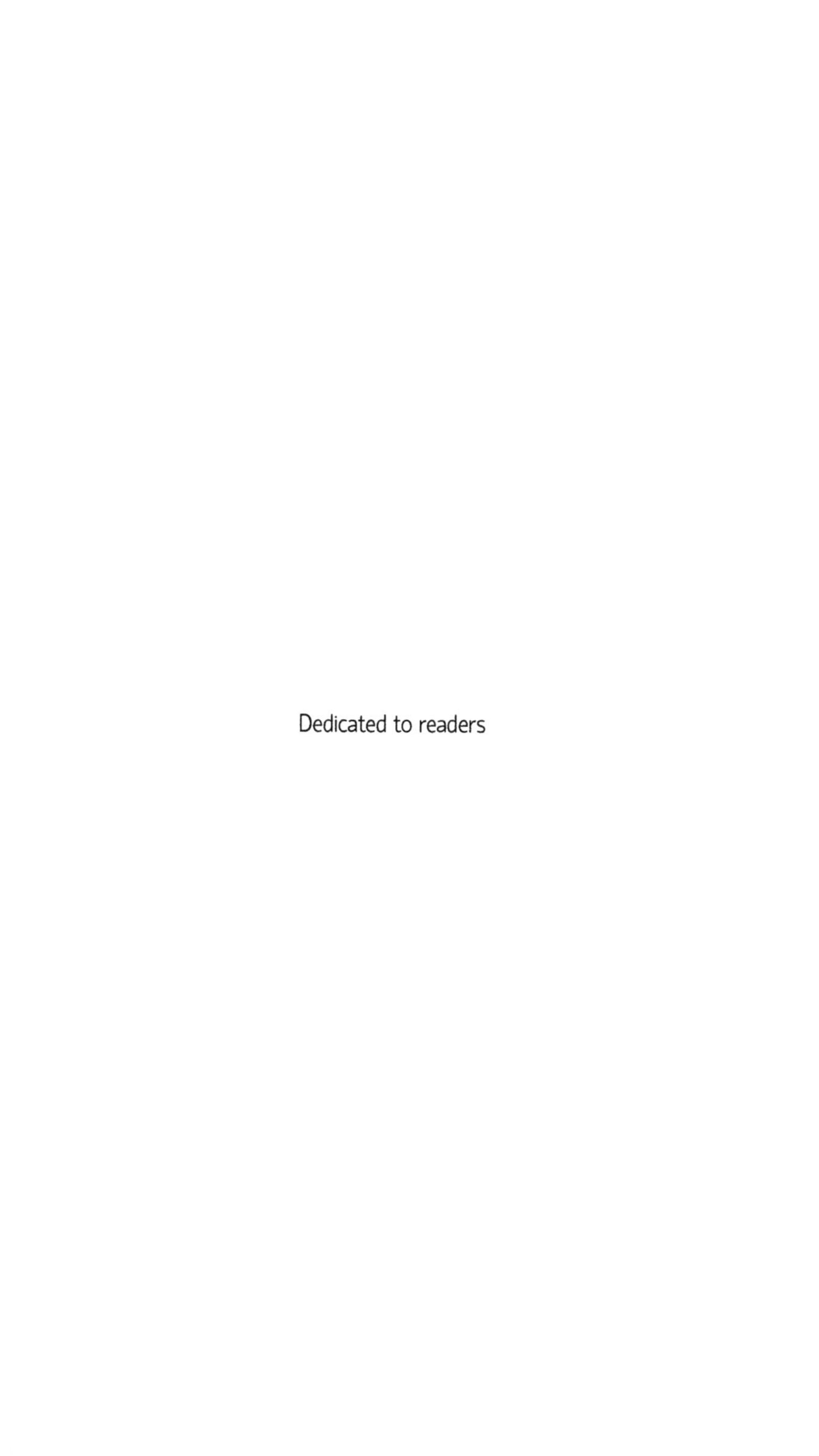

Dedicated to readers

Contents

CHAPTER ONE

AASHI

Abhinav hails from a poor family. Abhinav has three younger brothers named Kartik, Pankaj, Tanmay, and two younger sisters named Sachi and Sabita. Abhinav has completed his M.B.B.S. degree and all his siblings are studying in school. Abhinav wants to do his M.D. but due to his poor financial condition, he discontinues his study and sets up his private clinic. His parents plan his marriage with a beautiful girl named Prisha who hails from a rich family. Prisha's pet name is Aashi. Abhinav's siblings are very curious about whether Aashi will accept her new and not well-to-do family.

Abhinav tries his level best to keep Aashi happy. Aashi also never obliges Abhinav to help with his sibling's education but she is very tough and domineering at home and all his siblings have to adhere to her rules.

Aashi had many secret affairs with her ex-classmates and she continues it even after her marriage. Slowly, all of Abhinav's siblings understand her secret bedroom affairs which go on in her bedroom in absence of Abhinav. "We are financially benefitting from her and her rich dad, then, why simply envy her" ? they think and just overlook the matter. Aashi's dad pays for everything like Abhinav's sister's education, marriage, and all his brothers' education. So, they all get well settled in life and are grateful to their Aashi bhabhi. People who silently watch Prisha's activities chitchat about Abhinav on his back that he is weak and impotent which is why Aashi goes to other men for physical pleasures.

Out of this marriage, Aashi becomes pregnant and gives birth to a baby girl namely Varsha. When Varsha turns two, Prisha again gives birth to a baby boy namely Gaurav. After Varsha's birth, Prisha gradually reduces her time to meet her old boyfriends. She is strict and dominating to Varsha but very loving and liberal to Gaurav. In short, she shows extreme favoritism to Gaurav so Varsha secretly hates her. She wants to get out of this hell as soon as possible and finds a way to do so only after completing her graduation in science. Varsha gets a marriage proposal from a well-settled guy in Dubai, which she happily accepts to get out of that house and especially from her mother Aashi. Gaurav becomes a doctor like his father. Similarly, all his uncles and aunts get married and their children too grow up and settle in life. Gaurav's cousins too curse Prisha as she is very strict with them and their parents. Varsha herself curses her mom every day. Abhinav and Prisha get Gaurav married to a girl named Kiara. Kiara hails from a very rich family and is a homemaker by choice. Now, Abhinav and Prisha get free from all responsibilities. Varsha becomes a mother to a baby girl namely Babita. Gaurav and Kiara become proud parents to a baby boy namely Kanav.

Prisha seems happy and content in life unless she gets diagnosed with blood cancer at the age of 60. She suffers awfully for six months and atlast takes her last breath. Abhinav looks at her calm face and wishes her peace in death. "She was a very helpful woman", Abhinav's brothers

Kartik and Pankaj praise her. Sachi due to unknown reasons doesn't turn up while Sabita and Tanmay attend Aashi's funeral and pay respect to her. Varsha and her cousins who used to curse her also visit there to have a final look at their mother and wish her peace. They choose to forgive her now as she has become lifeless. "She enjoyed her past birth fruits but suffered because of her present life sins", few people exchange words about Aashi. Whether Abhinav knew about Aashi's affairs is still a mystery to everyone. Gaurav keeps crying like a baby seeing his mother on the deathbed. Although Aashi left everyone, her memories continue to cherish by everyone. The entire family continues to lead their life with unity and happiness.

CHAPTER TWO

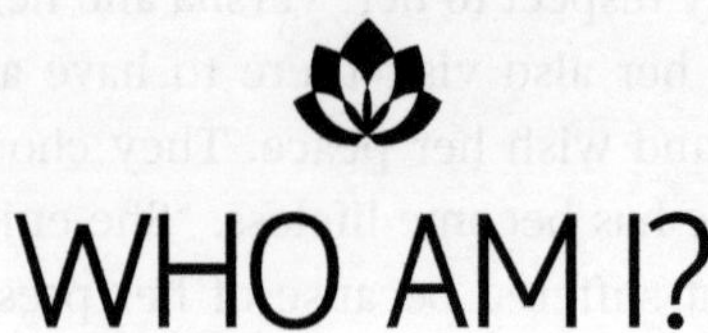

WHO AM I?

Takshak works in a private company in a small town. His work includes lots of traveling, which is why he can never spend time with his wife, Tapasya, who hails from a small village. The couple is devoid of a child even after five years of marriage. The problem is with Takshak, as he is suffering from the problem of infertility. The doctor had prescribed a few medicines for him.

Tapasya's poor and old father had gotten her married to Takshak after she had repeatedly failed her second-year graduation exam. Tapasya's mother had died due to Diphtheria when she was young.

"Shall we adopt a child? I feel very bored when you go to the office" many times, Tapasya had asked Takshak many times, but Takshak was not excited about adopting children.

But he pities Tapasya. He understands that Tapasya has a passion for singing, so he encourages her to take training in it from their village master. So, after clearing the junior exam in Hindustani classical, Tapasya and her friend Bhairavi seek blessings from Guru Nadeesh at his house to teach them further.

Nadeesh is a single person in that town who is well-versed in Hindustani classics. But unfortunately, he lives alone in his house as his wife expired recently, and the couple did not have progeny. Very soon, Tapasya becomes Nadeesh's favorite student because of her interest and devotion to music, and Bhairavi becomes jealous of seeing her progress. She had always considered Tapasya as her competitor more than a friend.

"I have come to know that it is Guruji's birthday next week. So what shall we offer Nadeesh, Sir, on his birthday?" asks Bhairavi.

"I will not be able to attend Sir's birthday as I am going to my native today. However, I will give you the money. Will you buy a gift for him?" asks Tapasya.

"Okay, I will do that", says Bhairavi.

Bhairavi's husband is not as rich as Takshak. He works in a small private firm. So Bhairavi buys a small gift for Nadeesh, and she keeps the 1000Rs that Tapasya had given for herself.

"I have bought and gifted a silver idol to Nadeesh, Sir. If you want to show me the receipt, I will do so", says Bhairavi.

"No. It's fine. No need of that", says Tapasya.

Tapasya goes to her village and returns after ten days. "Today, I am unable to attend the class as I have got guests in my house for a week", says Bhairavi.

"Don't worry, Bhairavi. Today, I am going to the class. I will give you the notes", says Tapasya.

Tapasya goes to Nadeesh's house for practice. After practice, Nadeesh prepares masala tea for Tapasya as she says she is catching a cold. After that, they chit-chat for half an hour.

"I couldn't meet you on your birthday. I am sorry Guru Ji," says Tapasya.

"I know that you had gone to your native place. The gift you both have given me is beautiful", Takshak points toward a small brass idol. Tapasya is now baffled.

"Bhairavi told me that she has been gifted a silver idol. Did she lie to me?" thinks Tapasya.

" Bhairavi, you are a liar. So you have gifted Nadeesh Sir a brass idol and kept the 1000 rupees I gave you for yourself"?

"Tapasya, I needed money, so I did like that. I will return your money in a few days", says Bhairavi.

"If you needed money, you should have asked me, and you should not have bluffed to me", says Tapasya irately.

"Why are you fabricating this matter? Leave it. Sometimes it happens."

"You always try to point out my petty slipups and buzz about them to everyone you meet. So I am at least just telling it to you straight away on your face and not in front of others, like how you do," says Tapasya.

Bhairavi goes away from there with tears in her eyes. "You are very proud of your beauty and talents. But, wait, I will take revenge for this mockery. You will have to pay for this Tapasya," thinks Bhairavi.

Now, she calls their common friend Neelima. Neelima also used to be Nadeesh's student earlier.

"How is your practice going on, Bhairavi?" asks Neelima.

"Practice is going well, but few amazing things are happening here."

"What is that, tell me?" "Neelima, do you know? Nadeesh and Tapasya are having a strange illicit relationship".

"Is it so? But it is hard to believe".

"I have seen them being intimate with my own eyes. Of course, I will not tell anyone, but you are my close friend, so I told you".

"Hmm, well, you can see that her husband is always out of the station, and they don't even have a child even after seven years of marriage. So, Tapasya might not be getting sexual pleasure from Takshak. This might have led her to fall in love with Nadeesh," says Neelima after thinking a bit.

"Yes. It is indeed like that. I will call you back later. Now, I have to go to the class," says Bhairavi.

"Okay, do give me the updates," says Neelima.

"Neelima, I know that you are a bigger gossip monger than me, and you never keep secrets to yourself, and you will tell this secret to everyone, and Tapasya, my revenge is completed", says Bhairvai in her mind.

One day Takshak meets his close relative, Roopa aunty, in a garment shop. She has come there for shopping.

"Takshak, how are you? How is Tapasya?" I need to talk to you. Come and meet me tomorrow at my place."

"Anything special, aunty?"

"You come and meet me tomorrow. I will tell you."

The next day Takshak goes to Roopa's aunt's house.

"Takshak, do you think sending your wife to Nadeesh' Sir for Classical training is okay? Please don't mistake me, but I heard people small talking about your family. So I hope you will take it positively and take suitable action for the well-being of your family."

"You are like my mother. I will think about this, aunty."

"Please have coffee, Takshak."

"No, aunty. Please excuse me."

Takshak goes back to his home without having coffee at his aunt's place.

"Takshak, I am preparing your favorite dishes for dinner today. I am very happy today as my performance was there in our nearby mandir, and the audience and even Guru ji appreciated my performance and hard work. It would be best if you had been there. Even you would have enjoyed it. Singing gives me immense pleasure. Wash your face and come. I will prepare coffee for you."
Takshak looks upset.

"Tapasya, you should stop going to class and concentrate on household chores," says Takshak as he drinks the coffee Tapasya brought for him.

"May I know what mistake I have made in my duties towards you? You know that singing is my only passion and goal in life. So what is compelling you to impose such a cruel order?"

"I just want you to obey my commands, or else I will divorce you", shouts Takshak

"Okay. I will do as you wish," says Tapasya with tears in her eyes, and she takes the empty glass from him.

“What happened Tapasya? Why are you not coming to class? "The next day, Bhairavi comes to Tapasya’s house and asks her with a winning smile on her face.

Tapasya observes that Bhairavi is trying to sham her.

"I am not well, Bhairavi. Kindly leave me alone. I don’t want to talk to anyone"

"I pity you, poor girl. Take care", says Bhairavi.

Tapasya comes to know that now Neelima is Roopa’s aunt’s new Neighbour. Takshak has no relatives in that town except Roopa’s aunty, and he respects her a lot. Tapasya knows that Neelima and Bhairavi are friends. So now she gets a rough picture of what might have made Takshak suddenly order her not to go to the training.

One day both of them were sitting together on the balcony bench and Tapasya speaks up. "I was wondering what made you order me to quit learning Sangeet. Now, I understand why you asked me to quit my Sangeet practice.

" I have taken a decision Takshak. I have been appointed as a caretaker in an orphanage in Hyderabad. I have decided that I will never come back to you. You are free to give me divorce or remarry anyone if you want. I often notice you are busy with your work, which is also your passion. I mean nothing to you. I don't know who I am and what is my life purpose. I was passionate about singing, but I could not pursue that skill as you were influenced by people's words rather than asking me the real truth.

I always wanted a child, but that is also not possible because of you, and you don't want to adopt a child. Now, I can see only one path: to serve people in need. So I have decided to become a mother to children seeking a mother's love. I could have continued learning music but I don't want Nadeesh Sir to be defamed because of me. Now, I know who I am and I have found a meaningful life.

I am going far away from this world full of jealousy and negativity to a new family where love and affection are valued, with many hopes. Good Bye, Takshak." Tapasya picks up her luggage which she has packed, and bids goodbye to Takshak forever without looking back at him.

Takshak tries to say something and tries to stop her, but he remains silent and unmoved. Tears start trickling down his eyes, but words are not coming out of his mouth.

Finally, he realizes his blunder and negligence towards Tapasya as he watches her go far from him FOREVER!!!!!

CHAPTER THREE

CHOICE

Saloni is an innocent looking sixteen years old, pretty girl. Her father, Nanjunda is a postman by profession in Guntur. Saloni's mother had expired when she was three years old because of an accident. Nanjunda wants Saloni to become an engineer and obtain a good job with a handsome salary. It is his only dream for the rest of his life.

Saloni is good at her studies. She secures ninety-five percent in the twelfth standard and obtains a seat in a reputed engineering college in Bangalore. The college is really good and there are chances that she might be immediately appointed to a good company, as soon as she obtains a degree from this college.

Nanjunda doesn't think twice and he gets Saloni admitted to that college. For the first time in Saloni's life, she has to stay away from her father. Nanjunda, gets Saloni admitted to a lady's hostel near her college.

"My child, study well and take care of your health. Call me if you have any problem. I will call you daily, "said Nanjunda with tears in his eyes.

In the first few days, Saloni feels left alone as her lifestyle is very much different from that of her classmates. Darpana and Tanya become her close friends. Saloni's dressing style also evolves from traditional to modern.

Slowly, Saloni starts enjoying her new life. She now dares to bunk class and go to malls with her friends. There they buy many fashionable outfits. Together, they go to a salon and get their eyebrows, spa, waxing, and highlights done.

All the boys are mad after these three girls. Saloni also chats with boys for hours before going to sleep. But she always feels lonely when Darpana and Tanya go to nightclubs with their boyfriends.

"Hey, Saloni, what happened? Why are you looking sad? Is it because I am going to the pub with Darpapna? " asks Tanya after seeing Saloni sitting sadly. By that time Darpana also comes back from class.

"You guys carry on. I don't want to become the third wheel"

"Hey, don't be silly. Come on, maybe you might meet your special someone there. So, get ready. Hurry up. Darpana, tell her"

"I am not looking for anyone right now" replies Saloni.

"See Saloni, even I don't like that, Ujjval much. I am just using him as my wallet. See how he has gifted me a new beautiful mobile phone. It is just to have fun and all this is common. Why are you becoming so serious? It is just for fun. Why are you acting so boring? Don't bore us. You are our best friend. Come on, get ready soon" says Darpana.

"Isn't it such a nice experience when somebody is ready to give their life to you? See Sagar does everything to please me" says Tanya.

"Leave her Tanya. Don't force her. Let's go. Let her sit here and study. Isn't that what she wants?" says Darpana.

"Of course! I will prepare for my unit test" Saloni tries to pretend. But she feels very lonely and sad after Darpana and Tanya leave her and go out to enjoy life with their boyfriends. Secretly she starts feeling that she too wants a boyfriend who cares for her and buys many gifts for her"

She calls Nanjunda and speaks to him but she becomes more bored after conversing with him. "Papa can just speak either about my studies or about what I ate today. Nothing more than that" mutters Saloni. While talking Nanjunda asks her to meet her uncle who is also a guardian to her in Bangalore.

That weekend Saloni goes to her uncle's place. Ram uncles' son Arun is also studying B.E but he is in his final year at a different college.

"Saloni, meet my friend Bhavesh. He is a model. He is very talented and Bhavesh, this is Saloni". Saloni and Bhavesh, both greet each other with a "Hello".

Bhavesh is a tall guy with six packs ABS, jet black hair and he is well groomed. He looks like a top model with very fine features. Saloni understands that he is a very rich guy as he shares many things about himself.

Saloni, even after going back to her room starts thinking about Bhavesh. "Why am I getting attracted to him?" at the same time, she gets a call from Bhavesh.

This conversation continues daily and very soon Bhavesh and Saloni realize that they are in love. They start hanging out everywhere.

One day Saloni is smiling while Darpana and Tanya are watching a sad scene.

"We are crying and what's making you sit and smile?" asks Tanya.

"Ah, nothing. I will be back. I am going to my classmate Ramya's room. See you", Saloni lies to Tanya that she is going to Ramya's room. She had a date with Bhavesh.

“Well Saloni, let me be the first to propose. I love you and I guess you too are loving me. Isn’t it Saloni?” asks Bhavesh.

“Well, your guess is correct”

"Are you sure Saloni? I am an orphan. My parents have left me their property but I don’t have anyone to tell that they are mine. All I have is my uncle and aunty who resides near my home. For the last five years, after my father left me here alone in this world, they are only everything to me. I should tell all this to you. Do you still love me?"

"Yes, Bhavesh. I have fallen in love with you and I don’t mind if you are an orphan"

"Saloni, today is my birthday and you have given me the best gift by accepting my proposal"

"Happy birthday, Bhavesh"

"I have brought a ring for you" Bhavesh gifts her a ruby studded ring and kisses her hand. Saloni had never received such an expensive gift in her life.

"Oh thank you, Bhavesh"

"I know you have to go now. Come we will have lunch and then I will drop you at your college"

Saloni is not at all able to concentrate in class. So she bunks the next period and goes back to her room.

"Darpana, Tanya I am in love. I too have a boyfriend. Today, he proposed to me and gifted me this ring. Do you know? He is very rich and handsome and he is a model” Saloni proudly displays and shows her ring to her friends.

“I had guessed that something like this is going on in your life when I saw you smiling all alone in the morning. Anyways I am happy for you, dear”

“You must see him. You will become jealous of my luck. He is so talented and handsome”

Tanya and Darpana both congratulate her.

Saloni loves her special new-found status of being a girlfriend to a guy. She feels great to have such a good-looking and rich celebrity kind of guy as a boyfriend.

Slowly, their love matures and they start kissing each other. Bhavesh takes her wherever she wants to go.

"Shall we go to lunch together tomorrow?" Bhavesh takes Saloni's hand in his hand and asks her.

He takes her to a five-star hotel and they have lunch together. After lunch, he takes her to his other bungalow, located in Indiranagar. "I come here often and spend some time" He shows her his cupboard. His childhood album and his collections.

Saloni is very excited to see such a big bungalow and his collections. Bhavesh observes her reactions and all of a sudden starts staring at her. Saloni is looking very beautiful in a black mini frock, black stockings, and black sandals. The dress hugged her body and enhanced her curves. She has straightened her hair. "She looks like an angel, in this dress," thinks Bhavesh.

" Saloni you are looking very beautiful today" Bhavesh gives a jaw-dropping expression. Saloni starts blushing after seeing his expression. "Would you like to have some Whisky?" Bhavesh opens the bottle.

"Not now"

"Just a glass. Not more than that. Come on"

"Ok, Just a little"

"You want it with ice or without ice?"

"With ice, please"

Saloni and Bhavesh chit-chat and have their drink together.

"You look so sexy and stunning. Saloni, you could be a heroine in any movie"

Bhavesh slowly touches her hair with his fingers and slowly moves it towards her neck and downwards from her neck to her chest. His touch is slow and filled with lust.

"Bhavesh, I think, I am not ready for this" Saloni resists.

Bhavesh kneels and takes his hands near her legs and removes her stocking and throws them on the floor.

"Your legs are worth showing"

The drink has made Saloni feel sexy and she looks at him seductively.

"I so damn want you now" Bhavesh moves his hands toward her thighs and starts rubbing the inner sides of her thighs. He stimulates her like an expert. Saloni loses control over her and moans.

"I love you, Saloni," says Bhavesh.

"I love you too, Bhavesh"

They spend their evening with lots of exploration and fun. That day they do lovemaking and they do it again and again for one year.

After one year, Bhavesh starts showing his true color. He starts avoiding Saloni. He never takes her calls.

Saloni takes an appointment with his manager and tries to meet him.

"Bhavesh, you never pick up the call. I even went to your home but it is locked all the time. Are you avoiding me? Your mobile is always switched off. Whenever I call your manager, he makes excuses by telling me that you are out of the station. I am very much tensed"

"Hey, cool down Saloni. You are getting tensed unnecessarily"

"I am tensed, Bhavesh. I am pregnant"

"What? Don't tell me. Didn't you use the safety method? How can you be so dumb?" Bhavesh slaps her.

"I had used safety methods. I also don't understand, what happened" Saloni starts crying.

"Now, we will have to get married, Bhavesh!"

"What nonsense! Are you joking? I am at the peak of my career. I can't marry you. You get the fetus aborted" shouts Bhavesh.

Saloni starts crying loudly.

"Take it easy, Saloni. Abort it. It is good for both of us, to do so"

"You are a cheater, you are a bastard! You spoiled my life. You will go to hell" shouts Saloni.

"You can say whatever you want, I didn't promise you anything so I am not a cheater, you got pregnant by your fault and it's up to you what you will do now. I am having lots of work, so now you can leave" Bhavesh opens the door for her.

Saloni goes back to her room with tears in her eyes.

"I am pregnant and Bhavesh is not comforting me. He is asking me to get the baby aborted. Please help me", Saloni tells Darpana.

"You are such an idiot. I had asked you to use his money, but you allowed me to use your body", Darpana screams at her.

"I am already so tensed, please don't scold me so much. You know that I am a sensitive person. I had loved him from the heart"

"I know a lady, who can help you. She will get your baby aborted, but you are already three months pregnant and it may be a risk to your life too".

"No Darpana, I can't kill my baby. I can't murder my baby"

"I don't know how to respond to this. Tell me if you need my help. I'm getting late for the class"

Saloni thinks for a while and calls her dad.

"Papa, I have to speak to you, please come and take me home"

"What happened, my child? Is everything alright"

"I want to see you. Please come. Don't question me anything. Please start immediately"

"I will leave today itself. Is everything alright?"

Nanjunda immediately books a ticket to Bangalore. He reaches Bangalore the next day morning.

"Saloni, my child. Is everything fine?"

"Papa, I need your help. I have committed a mistake" She tells everything that happened.

Nanjunda starts crying.

"So now do you want to abort the child?" asks Nanjunda.

"No Papa. I have made my CHOICE. I don't want to do so. I want to give birth to my child but I need your support, Papa"

"We will have to answer the society. You will be treated as a criminal in society. Think about that"

"I have not committed any crime. I was in love with him. I want to protect this baby. What wrong it has done?"

"I support your decision"

"Thank you, Papa. You are great"

Nanjunda takes back Saloni to his village. The villagers, make fun of Saloni and Nanjunda and sideline them from society. Many men ask Saloni to sleep with them too. Nanjunda and Saloni are not invited to any functions. But Nanjunda constantly supports Saloni and Saloni gives birth to a girl child. Saloni names her Rashmika.

Saloni and Nanjunda think about shifting to another village and suddenly one day Bhavesh comes there.

"Saloni, I came to know that we have a daughter. I have come to take you both back to my home. I am ready to marry you. I am sorry for all my mistakes. It was not intentional. At that time I was not in a condition to marry you. Please forgive me and give me a chance" requests Bhavesh.

Saloni is hugging her baby tightly, not allowing Bhavesh to see her face, and is crying continuously.

Nanjunda has come to have his lunch and overhears their conversation.

"Saloni, he is repenting for his mistake. Please forgive him" says Nanjunda.

Saloni does not speak a word.

"Let Rashmika get the love of her father," pleads Nanjunda.

Saloni looks once at Rashmika and once at her father and then slowly smiles at Bhavesh.

"yo hoo! Thank you, Saloni" Bhavesh kisses her.

He takes Saloni and Rashmika with him. Nanjunda is happy for his daughter.

CHAPTER FOUR

DEVADASI

"I want my daughter to become educated, and independent and marry a suitable boy. Please allow her to study", pleads Padma.

"Padma, don't forget that you are a Devadasi. Devadasis are not allowed to study or marry. Your daughter too will become a devadasi like you, which is my final decision. She will either become a devadasi or we will sell her in the red-light area", threatens Jagachandra, the zamindar of the village.

Padma is crying uncontrollably as she walks out of the zamindar's house.

"Padma, what happened? Why are you crying? Please share your problem with me. Don't be afraid. I will try to help you, "says Vaibhavi who sees Padma crying.

Vaibhavi has come to the village from Bangalore. She teaches the village children and the housewives to read and write as a part of her college project. Vaibhavi is a good-looking and intelligent girl. Many ladies and children in her village are influenced by her personality as she helps them not only to study but also in many other ways to tackle their day-to-day problems.

Vaibhavi consoles, Padma as she shares her painful story.

"Not only this much, but once the zamindar had asked me to abort my child when I was five months pregnant with his child, and I had to obey him. He had done this not only to me but to many other women. Nobody, not the government or NGOs, could help us," cries Padma.

"Don't cry, Padma. Times will change," assures Vaibhavi.

Vaibhavi teaches the children in the evening and the housewives in the morning. One day while teaching the ladies, Vaibhavi observes a girl of her age, crying and running in the road. Immediately, she rushes towards the girl. The other women follow Vaibhavi.

"Hey, what happened? Why are you crying? Please say something. What is your name?" asks Vaibhavi.

"My name is Ranjana. I am the daughter of Sunaina, a devadasi. Today, Jagachandra forced me to have sex with him. I had gone to his house to give him temple Prasad. He locked me in a room and raped me. I screamed so loudly, but nobody helped me," cries Ranjana.

"He has done this to many girls, but nobody could help it, "tells a lady standing over there.

"Who will dare to give a complaint against him? He has a mutual understanding with the police, politicians, and lawyers. All these influential people are also involved in many such crimes" says another lady.

"Ranjana, come with me. Today's class is over. You all can go to your home", declares Vaibhavi.

The next morning, the zamindar's wife Vasanthi picks up the newspaper and is shocked to see her husband's photo on the front page.

"Do you hear me? Your photo is published on the newspaper's front page," says Vasanthi.

Jagachandra who is still sleeping gets up from his bed and he too is shocked to see his photograph in the newspaper.

A few minutes later, the doorbell rings and Vasanthi opens the door. She is horrified to see the police.

"Call the zamindar, a girl named Ranjana has booked a case against him for raping her. We have come to arrest him," says the inspector.

Suddenly, Vasanthi gets pushed aside as Jagachandra opens the door wider and asks, "Don't you know about me? Hey, what's up?"

"Your story has been published in a newspaper and we will have to work on this case. The girl has got a report from a city doctor that she has been raped by you and she has come with proof. She did all this with the help of Vaibhavi, who is encouraging, our women, to speak out about their problems," says the police inspector.

"I will kill that bloody girl!" screams Jagachandra as the police arrest him.

"You can do nothing to me Jagachandra," says Vaibhavi. She is standing just outside the gate and steps up to see his arrest.

"I am a student of mass media communication. I hid from all of you. I was aware of the happenings in this village. My aunt Sharanya used to inform me of everything that happens in the village and I had come to start social reforms and stop your evil and abusive activities in this village. I am also a devadasi's daughter. Renuka Devi is my mother. I was acting as if I don't know her. My mother had told the villagers that I died during her labor, but she was educating me secretly in a hostel in Bangalore. I have come here with the help of my mother, to help the Devadasi's daughters and other helpless women like my mother. Today, I will bring an end to the sins. I had recorded videos and photographs of all the evil doings, you have committed. With the help of my media contacts, I published it in the newspaper. I also took help from the lawyer, a doctor, and the police from the nearby city."

Jagachandra and his wife are too shocked to speak out about anything. His wife retreats into her house, crying piteously.

"Inspector, what are you waiting for? Take him away and lock him up! Till now the Devadasis were afraid to open their mouth in front of the police. So, they were compromising not only with Jagachandra but many other so-called influential people of this village. My sisters, from today, you need not be afraid of anyone. "From today, there will be the pure Devadasi system, and children of Devadasis will study and get married if they are willing to do so. No one can force you into this system. You can call our NGO if you have any problems," says Vaibhavi, addressing the mob.

The village women gather around Vaibhavi and start clapping for her. They take her to Renuka Devi's house and praise her and Vaibhavi for helping them out.

CHAPTER FIVE

BEAUTY AND BECK

Albany is a very rich man. His wife, Ebele had died in a car accident a few years ago. The couple has three daughters Calandra, Daisy, and Beauty. Calandra and Daisy are selfish and greedy girls. Beauty is a beautiful, virtuous girl. Calandra and Daisy hate Beauty as she is gorgeous, kind, humble, and hardworking, unlike her sisters.

"Calandra, Daisy, and Beauty I have to go to France as I have some work there. I will come back in a month. Calandra, you are my eldest daughter and it is your responsibility to take care of Daisy and Beauty in my absence," says Albany.

"You don't worry, Dad, I will take care of my younger sisters," replies Calandra.

"What should I get for my darling daughters when I come back from France?"

"Dad, please get me a ruby-studded bracelet," says Calandra.

"Get me a violet color ball gown," says Daisy.

"Dad, I will pray that your journey is safe and you come back home safely. I don't want anything else just your safety," says Beauty.

"You are just trying to prove that you are unselfish "comments Daisy.

Beauty ignores her comment.

"Miss you so much daddy, goodbye. Have a happy and safe journey," Calandra, Beauty, and Daisy kiss their father and bid him goodbye.

Calandra and Daisy are not kind to their sister Beauty. They are jealous of her and hit her in their father's absence by making false accusations about her. Calandra curses her daily using foul language.

"Our mother died because of you Beauty. It would have been good if you were not born," says Daisy.

"Beauty, Calandra, and I want to eat Pumpkin Pizza tomorrow for breakfast. Go and buy pumpkins to prepare pizzas and don't forget to buy Pistachio ice cream. You can go as soon as Calandra returns from the live theatre show in half an hour. I am going out to a jazz club with my friends and I will have my dinner there," orders Daisy.

Beauty prepares fresh orange juice for Calandra and goes out to the market as soon as Calandra returns from the live theatre.

The two elder sisters would do nothing, while Beauty washed the dishes and swept the floors. Beauty's eyes are filled with tears and she eagerly awaits her father's return. After fifteen days, they get the news that the ship on which Albany was traveling has sunk due to a storm. All three girls are in shock and they cry upon hearing the news of their father's demise.

Suddenly Albany calls, "Calandra, I am not dead. I am alive,"

He tells her about his miraculous savior, "A gentleman named Beck, who had come there for scuba diving, has saved me. He is like a god to me. He was successful in saving my life after putting his own life in danger. I have taken shelter in Beck's place. I am still recovering and I will be back in a week," says Albany over the phone.

"Dad, we were very sad after hearing the news on the radio that your ship sank in the sea and not a single person in the ship was left alive. Even the police had confirmed that the ship in which you were traveling had sunk with no survivors. I am very happy to hear from you. Please come back home as soon as possible," cries Calandra.

Beck takes care of Albany and serves him day and night. Despite having many servants, Beck takes care of Albany personally. Beck is a millionaire and he lives alone in his bungalow. His parents passed away when he was quite young. He is an acid attack survivor. Three men sent by his business rivals had entered his bungalow while he was in his garden and had thrown acid on him a few years back. Beck's face, neck, and chest had gone affected by the acid attack. On the day, Albany's ship sank due to the storm, Beck had come near the seashore for scuba diving, in the early morning. He had seen Albany drowning and with great efforts, he had saved him from drowning.

"Dear Beck, you have saved my life and you took care of me like your father. How can I pay back your help, my son?" asks Albany.

"Not at all, sir, it is my pleasure to help you. But still, I have one request. You told me that you have three daughters. I am already thirty-three years old and I am still single. If you are willing to help me, can you get any one of your daughters married to me?" asks Beck.

"I will ask for their consent and will let you know for sure. Now, I seek your permission to leave," says Albany.

He sets on his journey towards his house. His mind is very confused and is in a dilemma after listening to Beck's proposal. He wants to pay back Beck's help during a crisis, but getting one of his daughters married to a disfigured man is a tough decision to take. His daughters are very happy to see him, they listen to the story and Albany shows them a photograph of Beck. The girls get scared of seeing Beck's photograph.

"Beck has saved my life. He is still a bachelor and is in search of a life companion. I would be happy if anyone of you agree to marry him, "says Albany.

"Sorry, Dad, I will not marry this beast. I agree that you should pay him back, but I can't sacrifice my life for that by marrying this ugly man," replies Calandra.

"I too can't marry a disfigured, horrible-looking person, just because he has saved your life, father," says Daisy.

"Dad, I will happily marry him, "says Beauty.

"Are you sure my child?" asks Albany.

"Yes, Dad, I don't have any problem marrying Beck," replies Beauty.

Albany kisses her and immediately makes plans to take her to Beck's place.

Beauty is very scared after seeing Beck, but she doesn't show her feelings in front of her father. She just wants her father to be happy.

"Sir, I want to speak with Beauty in private," says Beck.

"Beauty, do you love me?" Beck asks her once they are alone.

"Sorry, Beck but the truth is that I don't love you. I have agreed to marry you only for my father's happiness. I don't want him to suffer from guilt, "replies Beauty.

On hearing her thoughts, Beck feels happy that Beauty spoke the truth to him. He plans for them to spend time together and tells her father. "Sir, I will marry Beauty but I need one month. Till then you both can be my guests"

"I will have to go as I have just got the news that I am urgently needed in my city. Beauty will be your guest," says

Albany and leaves for home.

Beck takes care of Beauty very well. He treats her with a lot of kindness and he never speaks rudely to her. He cooks her favorite food for her and allows her to roam in his beautiful garden. He makes her bed and daily wishes her good morning and good night with a bouquet of fresh roses. Beauty is very impressed by his hospitality. He takes care of her every need even before she asks. He always makes her very happy.

"I am very ugly, but I love you do you too love me and marry me willingly!" beck asks this question Beauty every night and Beauty always replies "No, Sorry. Not willingly".

On being treated so lovingly like a queen, Beauty often thinks that only if he was not scary looking, she would have married him happily.

Slowly the days pass, Beauty gets addicted to Beck's love and now she is not scared of seeing Beck. She chats with her sisters often and she shows them photographs of her bungalow. Calandra and Daisy get very jealous after seeing the comforts and luxury Beauty is enjoying. Beck runs a successful IT business and owns a two-hundred-acre farmhouse and three bungalows near the beautiful Athie Valley. Calandra and Daisy get very jealous after seeing Beck's riches, but they successfully hide their emotions and show that they are very happy for Beauty.

They hatch a plan and lie to Beauty.

"Beauty, our father is very sick. He is not taking medicines properly. Please come home soon, "Calandra lies to her.

Beauty is worried and plans to go home immediately.

"Beck, my father is not well. I will have to go to my home," says Beauty.

"By all means, you can go to your home Beauty but please do come back. I love you very much. I will die without you. I can't live without you. Please remember that one life is waiting for you, "says Beck.

"Yes, I will be back as soon as possible. Take care, Beck, Bye," says Beauty.

Beauty rushes to her house. On reaching home she finds out that her father just had a common fever. Albany is very happy to see Beauty and asks her about Beck. He is happy to know that Beck is taking good care of Beauty. She spends twenty days with her father and sisters. The sisters repeatedly try in many ways to prevent Beauty from going back to Beck.

"I will act as if I have a stomach ache and at that time you call the doctor. You can bribe him and ask him to tell you that I am having a serious health problem and need proper care. You can request Beauty to stay here to assist you," says Calandra.

"I will do that and handle everything. Don't worry Calandra," says Daisy. They are unaware that Beauty has overheard their words. Beauty is sad to know that her sisters are jealous of her. That night Beauty gets a nightmare that Beck is not well and is suffering.

"I will have to go to Beck, Papa. I am scared that he is not well. I think, I love him," says Beauty.

"By all means, you go back to your Beck, my child. I will come and visit you soon," says Albany.

Beauty bids them goodbye and rushes to take a ship to meet Beck. She reaches his bungalow after two days and rings the doorbell, but Beck doesn't open the door. Instead, the housekeeper opens the door. Surprised, Beauty rushes to look for Beck. He has consumed a lot of alcohol and has become unconscious.

The housekeeper tells her that Beck has not been eating as well. She finds a photo of hers in his hand. Beck has written a poem on the backside of Beauty's photograph.

"I had seen only rain in my life, but it was you who brought a ray of sunshine into my life.
I had felt only pain, but it is you, who has brought happiness into my life.
Is beauty seen only through the eye?"
Don't souls recognize each other?
Dear Beauty, did you walk away from me?
I love you, dear Beauty,
You are all that I adore,
Have you forgotten me?
God, please send Beauty back to me, or else, please take my life,
I don't want to live such a life!
Dear Beauty, did you walk away from me?"

Beauty's eyes are wet. She realizes that she too has started loving Beck. She kneels near Beck and kisses him. Beck slowly opens his eyes.

"Have you come back, Beauty, or am I dreaming? I thought that you would never come back to me," says Beck and hugs her.

"Beck, I love you. I missed you so much all these days. I am in love with you," cries Beauty.

"Is that true Beauty? Will you marry me?" asks Beck.

"Yes. I will. I love you," Beauty once again kisses Beck.

Beck kisses her back. His eyes are wet with tears.

"Beauty, I had waited for this day. I am all alone. I was desperate to find my real love, one who could accept me, not by seeing my looks or riches, but by seeing my heart and that is the reason, I never took an interest to undergo any surgeries. My ex-girlfriend, Rose had abandoned me after the acid attack. Now, I have my real love and the soul mate of my life. I have seen that your love for father and me is so true. You are my perfect soul mate Beauty. I am very lucky to have a wife like you. Today, I will meet, my friend Earl, who is a surgeon, and start the procedure for any reconstructive surgery." says Beck.

Beck and Beauty get married a few weeks later. In a few years, Beck gets a new look after skin grafting and laser treatment. Beauty is very happy for her husband. In the meanwhile, Albany searches for a suitable proposal for Calandra and Daisy but they keep rejecting every proposal as their expectations are high and they are competing with Beauty.

"We are not so young now and maybe we will never get a suitable suitor," says Calandra after a couple of years of refusing suitors.

"We have ill-treated Beauty and we were jealous of her. God has punished us for our jealousy. I think at least now, we should stop envying her and marry a person who is suitable for us," replies Daisy.

Beck, after learning from Beauty that Albany is in search of suitors for Calandra and Daisy, helps Albany to find grooms for the sisters. Oliver and George are the sons of Beck's family friend and they agree to marry the sisters. Oliver and George knew these sisters and secretly loved them but were hesitant to propose to them since they refused so many suitors. Calandra and Daisy happily agree to Oliver and George's marriage proposal. Albany is happy for his daughters.

Soon Beauty announces that she is pregnant. The family is overjoyed for Beauty and Beck. After nine months, Beauty delivers a beautiful girl child. Beauty and Beck become proud parents to a baby girl and they name her

"Fairy" and they all lived happily ever after.

9 798889 860747

Printed by Libri Plureos GmbH in Hamburg, Germany